For my Papa Sam, the storyteller of our family.

You were always ready with a delightful tale or hilarious joke,
often breaking into laughter before you could deliver the punchline.
Your heart and soul live on within me and my children.
Your laughter rings clear in my memory even as you're bringing
smiles to Heaven, as you did here on Earth. I love you.

To my dear editor Karen,
I am so very grateful for your friendship and support.

This book is dedicated to anyone who has ever lost someone they loved dearly.
Their love is eternal. Their love never ends.

With love and gratitude,
Heather

This book is given with love

To

_____

From

_____

Author: Heather Lean

Developmental Editor: Karen "Hollywood" Austin

Illustrators: Nina Aptsiauri and Ali Khalid

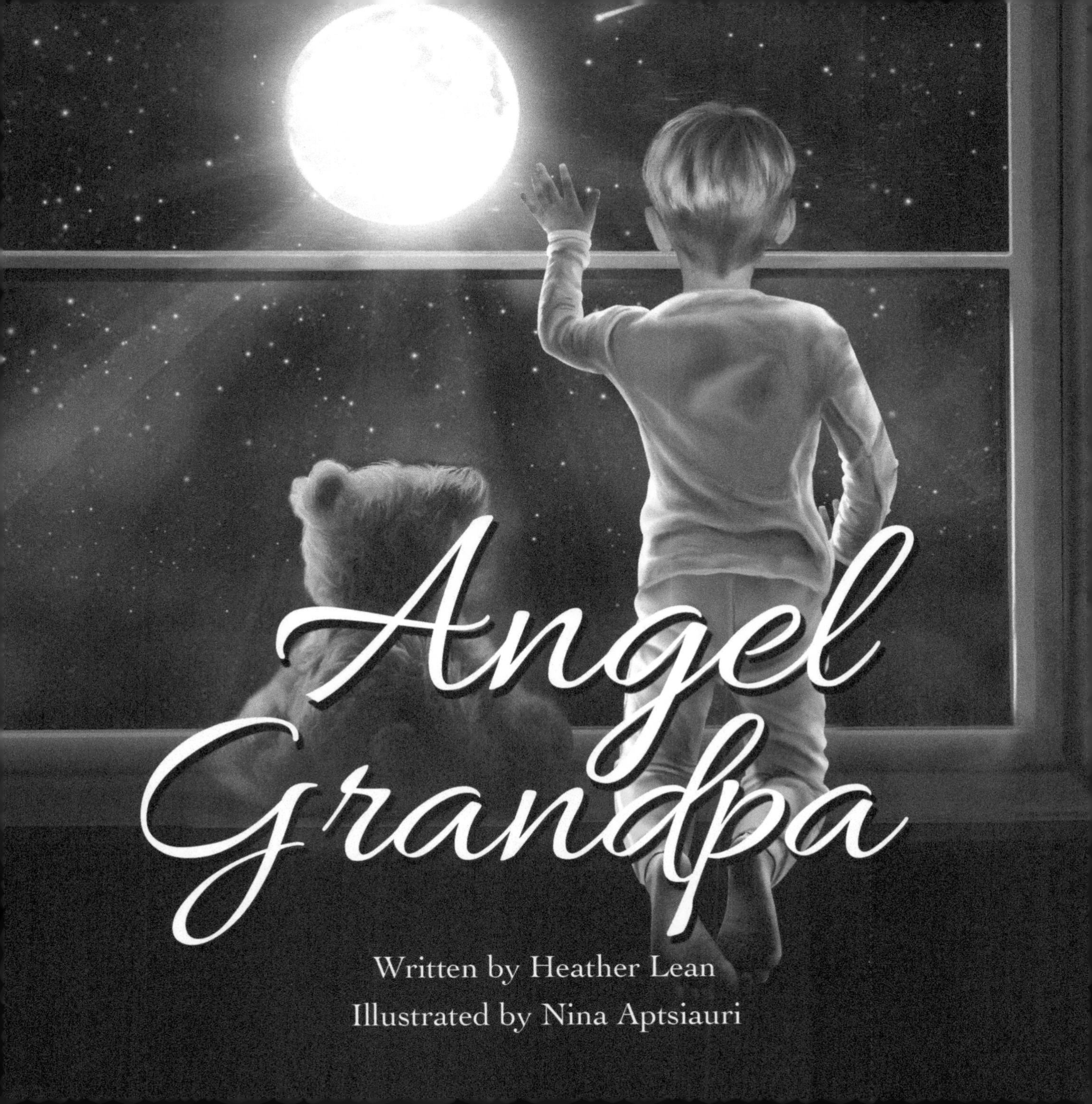

Angel Grandpa

Written by Heather Lean

Illustrated by Nina Aptsiauri

$\mathcal{F}$eel my love surround you

I'm watching as you play,

I am your angel grandpa

I'm never far away.

Sharing times together
Let me count the ways,
Laughing, skipping, dreaming
Through a sunflower maze.

Camping under moonlight
Our favorite kind of fun,
Hot dogs on a stick
And S'mores for everyone.

Your kite catches the breeze
And soars up in the sky,
My love shows up to meet you
Along with butterflies.

Climbing those tough mountains,
You always reach the top,
My spirit helps to guide you
So you won't have to stop.

When summer turns to autumn,
Pumpkins fill the patch.
It's hard to choose just one,
So bring home a whole batch!

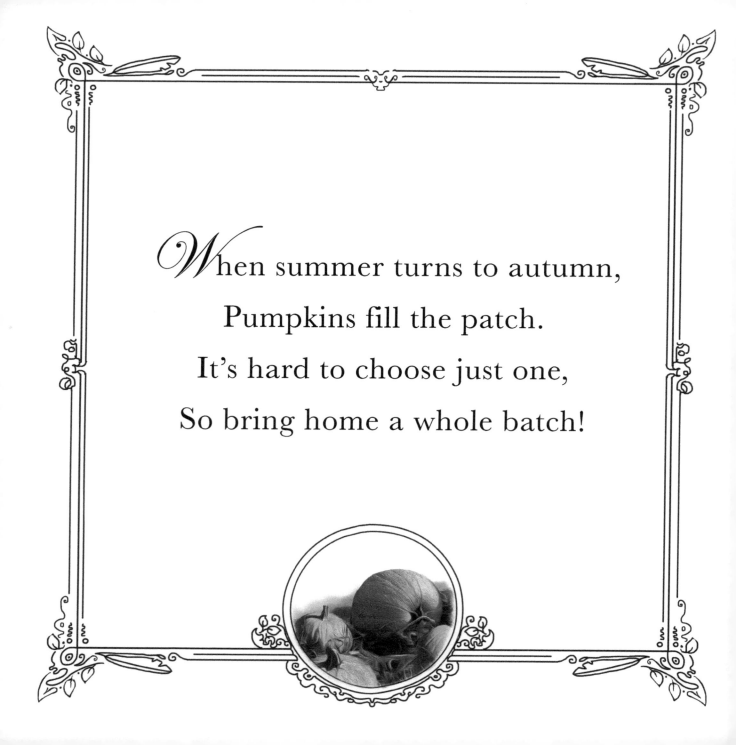

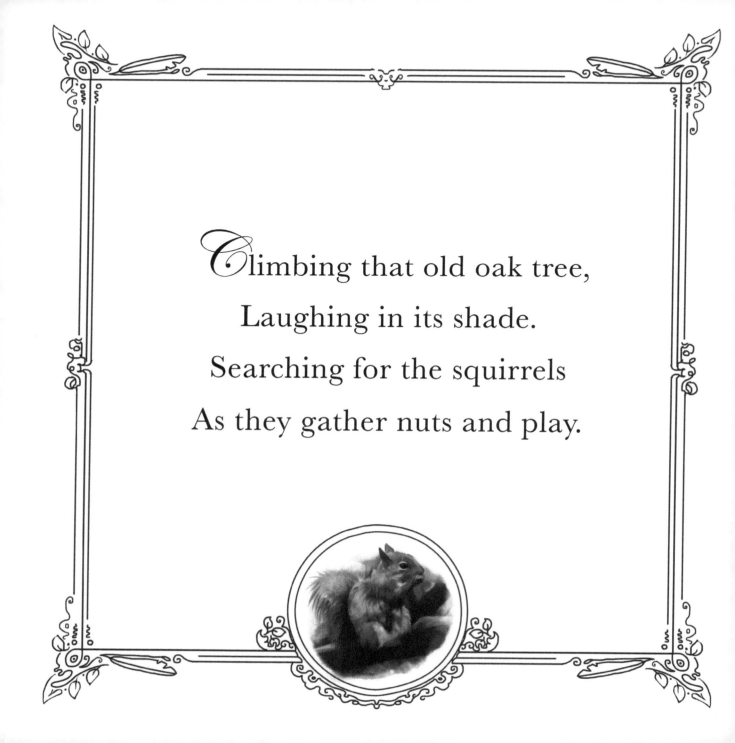

Climbing that old oak tree,

Laughing in its shade.

Searching for the squirrels

As they gather nuts and play.

Sitting on the sofa,

You try to stay up late.

Watching our favorite movies,

They always will be great.

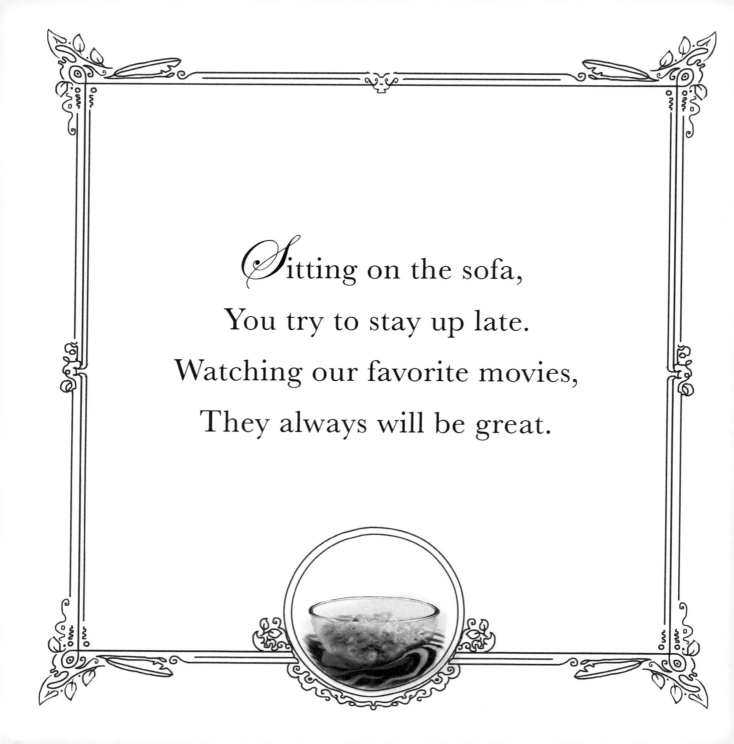

Splashing in the puddles
Of every fresh, new rain,
There's magic in the moment
When rainbows come again.

And when the evening comes,

Look up to find my star,

I will always be there

No matter where you are.

My love, my darling grandchild,

The apple of my eye,

My heart lives on within you

As all the years go by.

I Love You

Write a Memory

Write a message or special moment below
to remember your Angel Grandpa by.

_____

_____

_____

_____

_____

_____

Capturing Moments

Include a photo of your grandpa here.

About the Author

Heather Lean is an attorney and a mom of two. Her first book, Angel Grandma, was written after grieving the loss of her mother-in-law and her mother.

After writing this book, she found herself writing several others, and it was the spark that ignited her passion for writing children's books. All of Heather's books have a central theme of Love.

Heather resides in New York, where she enjoys spending time with her family, friends, and pets. She has four hens, three cats, and a puppy named Beau.

Other Books by the Author:

Angel Grandma

In fields of floating wishes
That rise above the dew,
I heard a tiny wish
Softly made by you.

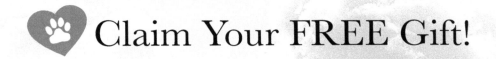 Claim Your FREE Gift!

Visit ➡ **PDICBooks.com/gift**

Thank you for purchasing Angel Grandpa, and welcome to the Puppy Dogs & Ice Cream family.

We're certain you're going to love the little gift we've prepared for you at the website above.

Lightning Source UK Ltd.
Milton Keynes UK
UKHW050949050323
418002UK00005B/36